SAMMY SPIDER'S
FIRST
PURIM

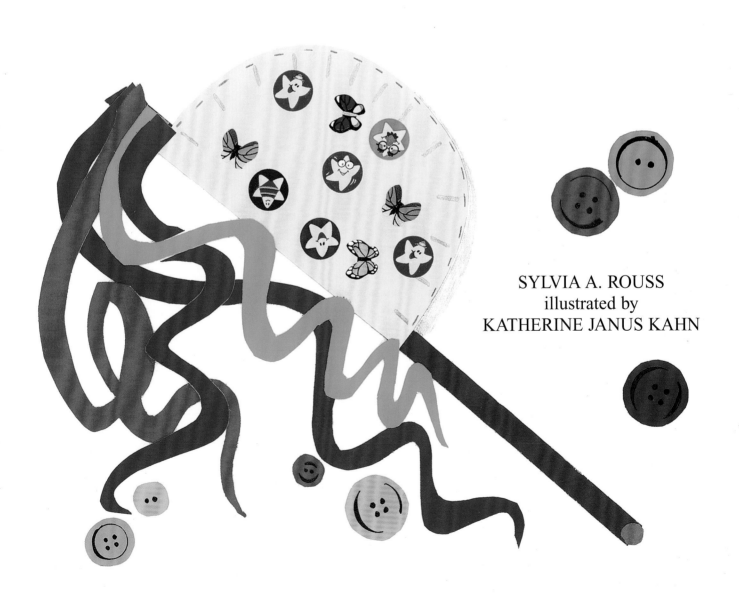

SYLVIA A. ROUSS
illustrated by
KATHERINE JANUS KAHN

This book is dedicated to the children and staff of the
Jewish Community Centers of Los Angeles,
the place where I began my teaching career,
my own children went to school and camp,
and where my husband has committed his professional life.
—S.A.R.

To Cary Jerome, the first of our next generation.
Be proud of your heritage
—K.J.K.

Library of Congress Cataloging-in-Publication Data

Rouss, Sylvia A.
    Sammy Spider's First Purim / Sylvia A. Rouss ; illustrated by Katherine Janus Kahn.
        p.   cm.
    Summary: A young spider wants to join in as Josh and his mother bake hamantaschen, make a costume, and spin
the grogger in celebration of Purim.
    ISBN-13: 978–1–58013–062–2 (pbk.)
    ISBN-10: 1–58013–062–3 (pbk.)
    [Purim—Fiction. 2. Jews—United States—Fiction. 3. Spiders—fiction.] I. Kahn, Katherine, ill. II. title.
    PZ7.R7622 Sane 2000
    [E]—dc21   99-056681

Published by KAR-BEN PUBLISHING, a division of Lerner Publishing Group, Inc.
241 First Avenue North, Minneapolis, MN 55401   1-800-4KARBEN   www.KARBEN.COM

Printed in the United States of America
2 – PC – 8/10/11

WHRRRR

crunch

Sounds

sNIPssshsssh

HMMMMMMM

C·R·ACK

SNIP, SNIP, SNIP.
Sammy Spider opened one sleepy eye
as he peered down from his web.
Beneath him at the kitchen table,
Josh was using scissors to cut
a shiny piece of fabric.

SNIP SNIP SNIP SNIP

Now Sammy was
wide awake. "MOTHER,"
he shouted. "What is Josh doing?"
A startled Mrs. Spider woke from a sound sleep.

ssh ssh sssh sssh

"Sammy, can you please speak a little more softly?"
She gazed downward.

"He's making a costume for Purim. Josh will wear it tonight when the family goes to synagogue to hear the story of how Queen Esther saved the Jewish people from wicked Haman."

"Can we go to synagogue and hear the story too, Mother?" Sammy asked.

"Silly little Sammy,"
said Mrs. Spider.
"Spiders don't go to synagogue. Spiders spin webs."

BANG went the cupboard door, drawing Sammy's attention to the kitchen counter, where Mrs. Shapiro had placed a bowl, flour, sugar, oil, eggs, and a can of poppy seed filling.

"MOTHER!" Sammy yelled. "What is Mrs. Shapiro making?"

"Please use your soft voice," Mrs. Spider reminded Sammy. "Mrs. Shapiro is baking delicious three-cornered cookies called hamantaschen. She will put some into baskets, and Josh will deliver them to the neighbors."

"Can we bake hamantaschen, too?" asked Sammy.

"Silly little Sammy," answered Mrs. Spider. "Spiders don't bake hamantaschen. Spiders spin webs."

CRACK! Mrs. Shapiro broke the eggs and added them to the bowl. WHIR went the beaters. Sammy watched Mrs. Shapiro roll the dough and cut it into circles.

He listened to the hum of the can opener as she
opened the can of poppy seed filling, put a spoonful
in the center of each circle, and pinched three corners
to make a triangle.

Suddenly Sammy heard SQUIRT, SQUIRT, SQUIRT coming from the kitchen table. Josh was squeezing glue from a bottle onto a folded paper plate. "MOTHER!" screamed Sammy. "What is Josh doing now?"

"Sammy, please speak quietly," said Mrs. Spider. "Josh is making a noisemaker called a grogger. Tonight he will twirl and spin it whenever he hears Haman's name."

"Can I spin a grogger, too?" asked Sammy.

"Silly little Sammy," said Mrs. Spider. "Spiders don't spin groggers. Spiders spin webs."

Sammy lowered himself onto a strand of webbing to get a closer look.

He listened to the soft tinkling of the glitter as Josh sprinkled it onto the glue.

Josh filled the grogger with buttons.

As he reached for the last handful,
Sammy scurried inside the grogger.
Just then he heard a loud CRUNCH
as Josh stapled the grogger shut.

Josh gave the grogger
a practice shake . . .

. . . and the buttons rained down on Sammy.

From inside the grogger Sammy shouted, "Mother!"

HONK! Mr. Shapiro beeped the horn as he pulled the car into the driveway. "Dad's home," called Mrs. Shapiro. "Time to get ready for services." Josh left the grogger on the table and ran to put on his costume.

"Mother," Sammy shouted again.

Mrs. Spider couldn't see Sammy but she could hear him.

"Where are you?" she called.

"I'M HERE, MOTHER!" Sammy hollered.

"INSIDE THE GROGGER!"

Mrs. Spider hurried
over to the grogger.
Luckily she noticed that
one of the staples was loose.
She tugged and pulled until
finally it came out.

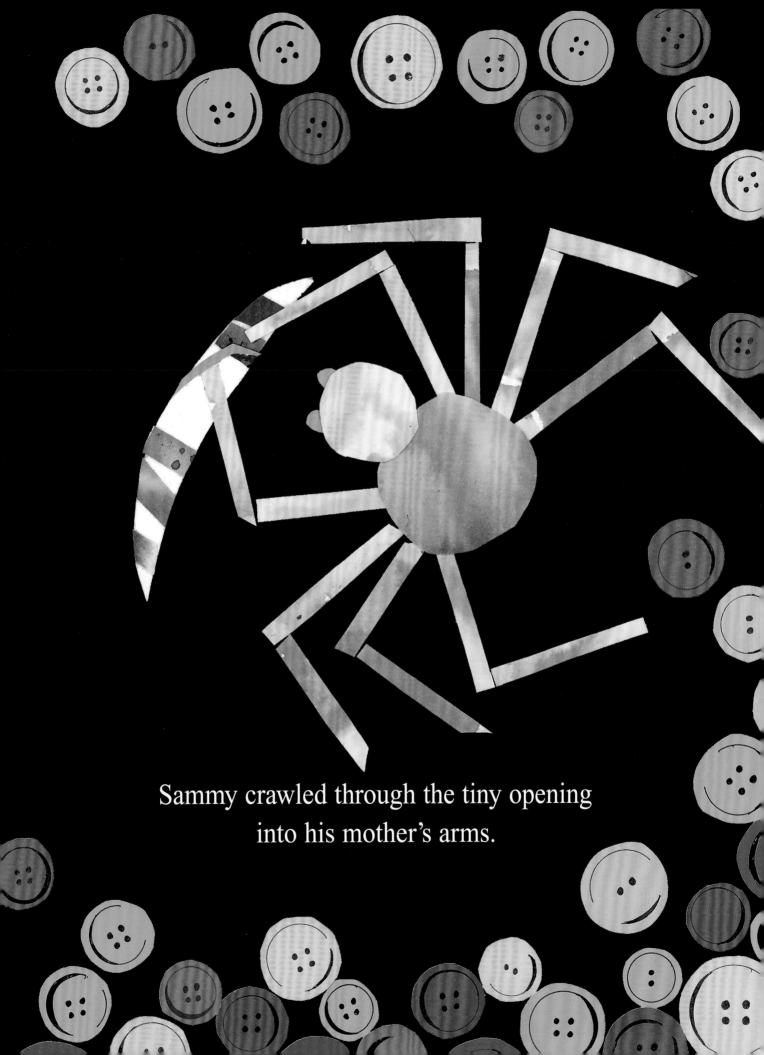

Sammy crawled through the tiny opening
into his mother's arms.

Just then Josh came back into the kitchen, grabbed his grogger, and dashed out.

"OH MOTHER!" squealed Sammy. "Don't you wish we could have a grogger for Purim?"

Mrs. Spider laughed.
"We don't need a grogger.
We have you, Sammy.
You are our
VERY OWN NOISEMAKER!"

ABOUT PURIM

Purim is one of the happiest holidays of the Jewish year. It recalls that long ago, in the city of Shushan, Persia, a wicked man named Haman tried to kill the Jews. They were saved by a Jewish queen named Esther and her cousin Mordecai. The story of Purim is told in the Biblical book of Esther. On the holiday, families dress up in costume and go to the synagogue to hear the story read from a scroll called a Megillah. When the name of the villain, Haman, is read, they whirl noisemakers (called groggers) and make lots of noise, to drown out his name. A special Purim treat are hamantaschen (a Yiddish word meaning Haman's pockets), three cornered cookies filled with poppy seeds or jam.